NICHOLAS NICKLEBY

Written by **Charles Dickens**
Illustrations by **Ludovic Salle**

KB086163

스푼북

Golden Square

In a small cottage, nestled between the rolling green hills and seaside towns of Devon, lived the Nicklebys.

There was Mr Nickleby, his wife Mrs Nickleby, their daughter Kate, and their son, Nicholas Nickleby.

Nicholas and his sister had a happy childhood in the countryside. For them, every morning felt like the first day of summer. It was never too cold to play outside nor too hot to read by the fire. They could not – even if they tried really hard – think of a better place to live than Devon.

Their uncle, Ralph Nickleby was very different from his brother, Mr Nickleby. He was not married, he had no children and had no friends either. He preferred it that way, he said.

Ralph lived in a fine house in Golden Square, right in the middle of London. Like many very rich men, Ralph loved nothing more than money. He loved saving his money, counting his money and, above all, making more money. To do this, he would lend large sums of money to struggling people and force them to pay it back with extra on top. Secretly, he looked forward to the day when they had to admit that they could not pay him back. When this happened, Ralph would take their houses and businesses as payment for their loan.

Sadly, when Nicholas and Kate were only teenagers, their father died. To make matters worse, his death left them without a penny to their names. So Mrs Nickleby and her children decided to move to London.

Mrs Nickleby wrote to ask Ralph for help. They were his family, so she thought that, surely, he *must* care for them. She was wrong.

Ralph employed an assistant called Newman Noggs. Newman was a good man, with a kind heart.

One morning, Newman knocked on the door of Ralph Nickleby's

office.

'Come in,' a voice boomed from inside. Newman turned the handle and stepped through the ornately carved doorway.

'I have a letter for you, sir,' he said to Ralph, who was sat at his desk, hunched over a pile of paperwork. Newman handed Mrs Nickleby's letter to Ralph with a sympathetic nod. The envelope had a black border and was sealed with black wax. These were signs that the

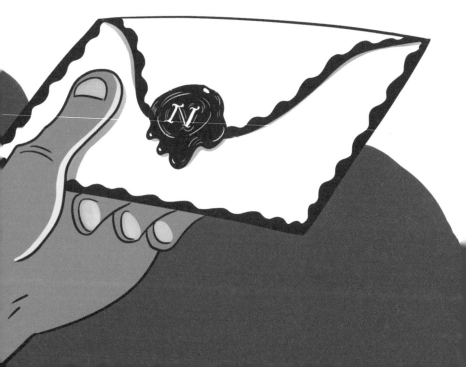

letter inside was about someone's death.

Ralph recognised the handwriting on the envelope.

'Newman,' he said, 'There's no need to look sad. I would not be surprised or horrified if my brother were dead.'

'I did not think that you would,' said Newman, quietly.

'Why not?' snapped Ralph.

'You never are surprised,' said Newman, 'that's all.'

Ralph Nickleby snatched the letter, tore open the envelope and read it.

'He *is* dead,' said Ralph, trying to look upset. 'Dear me! Well, that is sudden.'

Newman sighed. He was not fooled by Ralph's acting.

'Did he have children?' he asked.

'Yes, children alive and a widow too,' said Ralph. 'And all three of them are in London. What a nuisance.'

Finally, after a great deal of moaning, Ralph Nickleby left his home in Golden Square. He walked to the small house where Mrs Nickleby was staying with Nicholas and Kate.

He was not pleased to see his sister-in-law, the widowed Mrs Nickleby. He was not pleased to see his niece Kate, or his nephew Nicholas either.

In fact, of the three people now stood in front of him, Ralph disliked Nicholas the most. Maybe it was because the young man reminded him of his brother.

'What a sorry-looking bunch you are,' Ralph muttered under his breath. Then he looked up and without even saying a proper "hello", asked Nicholas, 'Have you ever done any work? Ever made any money?'

'No,' said Nicholas.

'No, I thought not!' said Ralph. 'This is the way my brother brought up his children: lazy.'

Saddened by Ralph's cruel remarks and the reminder of her dear husband's death, Mrs Nickleby started to cry. Kate was quiet. Nicholas, however, began to grow angry with his uncle.

'Are you willing to work?' Ralph asked.

'Of course I am,' snapped Nicholas.

'Then see here,' said his uncle.

Ralph took a newspaper from his coat pocket. He pointed to a small advertisement.

It said:

Mr Wackford Squeer's School
Dotheboys Hall
in Yorkshire
provides boys with food, lodging,
clothing and a fine education.
Mr Squeers is looking for a good
young teacher to join his staff.
Enquire at
the White Horse Inn, London.
Yearly salary: 5 pounds.

'If you're looking for work, nephew, there it is – a teaching position,' said Ralph Nickleby.

'But five pounds is not much for a year's work,' said Kate. 'And Yorkshire is so far away.'

'Hush, Kate, my dear,' said Mrs Nickleby. 'Your uncle knows best.'

'What will happen to my mother and sister if I go to Yorkshire?' asked Nicholas.

'I'll see to them,' said Ralph sharply, before clearing his throat and starting again.

'I'll look after them, I mean,' he said in a surprisingly soft voice. 'But only if you take that job.'

Nicholas agreed and went with his uncle to the White Horse Inn. There they found Mr Wackford Squeers.

Mr Squeers was a short, round man. His face was twisted and scarred on one side as though he had once wandered much too close to a fire. He didn't look like any teacher or headmaster that Nicholas had ever seen. With him were a couple of sad-looking boys. They were new pupils at Dotheboys Hall.

Mr Squeers was taking them from London to Yorkshire.

Mr Nickleby and Mr Squeers seemed to know each other. They nodded at one another, stood up and walked over to a corner of the inn. After a few minutes of private whispers, the two men returned.

'The job at Dotheboys Hall,' said Mr Squeers in a gruff voice, 'is yours.'

As they left the White Horse Inn, Nicholas turned to his uncle. 'Thank you for finding me the job,' he said. 'I shall never forget this kindness.'

'Make sure you don't,' said Ralph.

'The coach leaves here at eight o'clock tomorrow for Yorkshire. Be on time.'

Ralph handed Nicholas a stack of papers. 'Take these back to my house for me,' he said. 'I have some business to take care of.'

Nicholas did as he was told.

Upon entering the house in Golden Square, he was met by Newman Noggs. Newman was surprised to meet Ralph's nephew. He was more surprised still when Nicholas told him that he was going to Dotheboys Hall and that he was "grateful for the opportunity".

'Dotheboys Hall, eh?' said Newman, rubbing his red nose.

'You're *grateful* to Mr Nickleby for sending you to work at Dotheboys Hall? Well, well.' Then he sighed and patted Nicholas on the shoulder.

If Nicholas hadn't known better, he might have thought that Newman Noggs felt sorry for him.

Dotheboys Hall

Mrs Nickleby and Kate said goodbye to Nicholas the next morning at the White Horse Inn. Ralph Nickleby was there too, though he was not bothering with any emotional goodbyes.

Mr Squeers appeared with the two sad boys, who looked more like prisoners than pupils. They were, according to Mr Squeers, the Snawley brothers.

As Nicholas climbed up to his seat on the coach, he felt someone tugging at his leg. It was Newman Noggs. He pushed a letter into Nicholas's hand.

'What's this?' asked Nicholas.

'Hush!' said Newman Noggs, pointing to Ralph Nickleby. 'Don't let him hear you. Just take it. Read it.'

Confused, Nicholas put the letter in his coat pocket and waved goodbye to his family.

It was a long, cold journey from London to Dotheboys Hall in Yorkshire. Nicholas and the miserable Snawley brothers travelled on top of the coach. They huddled up against the wind and snow.

Mr Squeers, meanwhile, sat inside the coach. The seats there cost more than the open seats up top.

Eventually they arrived at a long, drab-looking house on the Yorkshire moors. Nicholas, Mr Squeers and the Snawley brothers got down from the coach and watched it trundle away.

'Is *this* Dotheboys Hall?' asked Nicholas.

Mr Squeers laughed.

'We call it a "hall" down in London because it sounds better, Nickleby,' he said. 'Anyone can call their house a

hall or a castle or a palace, can't they? There's no law against it.'

Mr Squeers rapped his stick on the locked wooden gates in front of the house. After a few minutes, a limping figure appeared on the other side and unlocked them.

'Is that you, Smike?' said Squeers.

'Yes, sir,' replied the limping boy.

'Why did it take you so long to get here?'

'Please, sir, I fell asleep by the fire.'

'A fire! Who lit a fire? Where?'

'In the kitchen, sir,' said Smike.

Mr Squeers suddenly grew very angry. He struck at Smike three times with his stick. The boy yelped but didn't move. A single silent tear escaped Nicholas's eyes – he had never seen such cruelty before.

Slowly, they all walked towards the dreary house.

This was the beginning of Nicholas's unhappy time at Dotheboys Hall. He soon saw that it was a truly terrible place.

There were about thirty boys in the school. They were clothed in rags, fed measly scraps of food and taught almost nothing. They were terrified of Mr Squeers. He threatened them and often beat them.

These unfortunate boys, like the Snawley brothers, were there because their parents didn't want them at home. Putting them in Dotheboys Hall was like sending them to outer space – somewhere so far away and cut off from London that they could pretend their children did not exist.

Mr Squeers was helped by his wife. Mrs Squeers was, if anything, even worse than her husband. Every morning she gave the boys spoonfuls of bitter treacle to keep their appetites down, so they wouldn't eat too much food.

Nicholas would have left straight
away if he could. But he knew that
his uncle Ralph would only take
care of his mother and sister if he
stayed at Dotheboys Hall. That was
the agreement, and he could not let
his family down.

One cold evening, crouching by the tiny fire, Nicholas found the letter from Newman Noggs that he had tucked into his coat.

He began to read it.

Newman wrote that if Nicholas ever needed shelter in London, then he should go to him. He gave his address – a single room in Silver Street, near to Golden Square.

Nicholas felt tears prick his eyes for the second time since his arrival at Dotheboys Hall. Just from this letter, Newman Noggs had shown that he was more a friend to Nicholas than his uncle Ralph had ever been. As he was folding the letter away, Nicholas noticed a sudden movement in the corner of his eye. It was Smike, the boy who had unlocked the gates.

He was trying to sneak closer to the fire. When he saw Nicholas looking at him, Smike shrank back in fear.

'Don't be afraid,' said Nicholas. 'Are you cold?'

'N-no.'

'You are shivering.'

'I am not cold,' Smike said quickly. 'I am used to it.'

'Come closer,' said Nicholas. 'Take what little warmth there is.'

'Th-thank you, sir.'

From that moment on, Smike became devoted to Nicholas.

Smike was older than the other boys. He was almost a young man. Nicholas learnt that he had been left at Dotheboys Hall many years before.

No one paid Smike's fees now. But Squeers kept him on because he was useful at doing odd jobs around the school and outside in the freezing cold. Smike worked hard, but in return he received only mean words and the occasional kick.

Nicholas felt sorry for all the boys in the school, but he felt especially sorry for Smike.

A GREAT ESCAPE

One morning, Smike disappeared. Without a word of warning, he had run away from Dotheboys Hall!

Mr and Mrs Squeers set out in different directions to hunt him down. After a full day of searching it was Mrs Squeers who found him. She brought Spike back, tied up like an animal in the back of her cart.

Mr Squeers called the whole school together.

He was going to punish Smike in front of everybody, including Nicholas. He was going to make an example of him.

Smike was dirty. His already-ragged clothes had fresh holes and tears. His teeth chattered with fear and cold, and his face was smeared with dirt.

Squeers grasped Smike's arm firmly with one hand and raised his cane in the other.

'Stop!' cried Nicholas.

He marched forwards.

Squeers lashed his cane at Nicholas and cut him across the face.

Nicholas seized the cane and turned it against the hated schoolmaster. He could not stand this cruelty anymore.

Squeers fell to the floor as the boys looked on in amazement.

Mrs Squeers shrieked. Clenching her fists, she rained blows on

Nicholas's back.

But Nicholas threw her off.

Grasping Smike's hand, Nicholas half walked, half ran from the schoolroom.

Within minutes, the pair were moving along the road away from the dreadful Dotheboys Hall.

Nicholas had barely had time to grab his few possessions before Mr and Mrs Squeers came running after him. But poor Smike had nothing more than the clothes on his back.

Tired, hungry and struggling with Smike's limp, it took the two friends many days to reach London. Nicholas had a little money. It was enough to buy some food and sometimes a bed in a cheap inn. When the inns wcrc too cxpcnsive, however, the pair would find a barn or a deserted cottage to sleep in.

Eventually, they reached Silver Street in London and knocked gently on the door of Newman Noggs. Newman seemed very pleased to see them. He gave them shelter in his little room and shared his dinner with them.

A Close Call
for Kate

If Nicholas believed that his uncle Ralph would *really* look after his mother and sister, then he was wrong.

It is true that Ralph Nickleby found them a house to live in – a small, dark and dirty place down near the River Thames. It is also true that he found Kate a job with a dressmaker called Madame Mantalini.

But Madame Mantalini grew jealous of Kate because she was young and beautiful. She did her best to make Kate's life miserable.

Nicholas had no idea how horrible Kate's life had been since he had left.

When he returned to London with Smike, he was overjoyed to see his mother and sister again.

But while he and Smike had been making their way to London, Mr Squeers had been writing to Ralph Nickleby, telling him about the events at Dotheboys Hall. Naturally, Mr Squeers made everything sound much worse than it was. He even accused Nicholas of stealing Mrs Squeers's jewellery.

'It's not true!' Nicholas cried. But his uncle would not listen to him. He said that if Nicholas did not leave London immediately, he would have nothing more to do with Mrs Nickleby or Kate. He would turn them out of their small, dirty house and make sure that Kate lost her job with Madame Mantalini.

Nicholas had no choice.

He set off with Smike, planning to go to Portsmouth. He thought that they might be able find work together on a ship, and perhaps leave England and their horrible mcmories behind.

Before they reached Portsmouth, however, Nicholas and Smike met a company of travelling actors. The company was run by a large, cheerful man called Vincent Crummles. He, his wife and the other actors travelled from town to town putting on plays. Even the Crummles's young

children took part in the plays. Mr
Crummles was always on the lookout
for new faces. He invited Nicholas
and Smike to join their group.

Nicholas had never acted before, but soon found that he was rather good at it. He was cast as Romeo in the company's retelling of William Shakespeare's *Romeo and Juliet.* Smike also had a small part to play, which he adored. It seemed that the pair were finally happy.

But, like most good things, this soon came to an end. Nicholas received a letter from Newman Noggs, who had been keeping an eye on Kate and Mrs Nickleby. The letter told Nicholas that he must return to London straightaway. It was an emergency.

It seemed that poor Kate had been caught up in the nasty side of her uncle's business. Ralph knew that his niece was beautiful and he often used her beauty to attract customers. One of these customers was a young nobleman.

Each time he would visit to borrow money, Ralph would tease him with the idea that he could, one day, marry Kate. Every time he did this, the nobleman would return to borrow more money. And the more moncy he borrowed, the more he paid back. This meant that Ralph was becoming richer and richer thanks to his niece.

Kate was very upset about this. She wanted to speak to her mother about it, but it was no good. Mrs Nickleby thought that Ralph knew best, no matter what he did. And when it came to a nobleman wanting to marry her daughter ... well, Mrs Nickleby quite liked that.

Not knowing where to turn, Kate told Newman Noggs about her uncle and the nobleman. 'Do not worry, dear Kate,' Newman said as he passed Kate a handkerchief to dry her tears. 'We'll sort this out. I'll write to your brother at once.'

After reading the letter, Nicholas
and Smike said a speedy farewell
to the Crummles family and set off
once again for London.

Nicholas marched straight into his
uncle's home in Golden Square, too

angry to politely knock at the door.
He strode – muddy boots and all –
into his Ralph's office.

'How could you treat Kate this
way?' he roared. 'She is your niece!
Not an advert for your business!'

Ralph's face hardened. 'I have done nothing wrong. Business is business. What does it matter if a foolish young man is attracted to Kate? It is not as if I sold her on the market like a dead fish!'

Nicholas could not stand it any longer. He told Ralph that neither he, his mother nor Kate would have anything more to do with him.

So Mrs Nickleby and Kate were forced to leave the small, dirty house by the Thames, and Kate lost her job with Madame Matalini.

They were safe from Uncle Ralph,

but where could they go next?

THE CHEERYBLE BROTHERS

Everything started to change for Nicholas and his family. And it changed for the better.

Nicholas was looking at the job notices in the window of a local office.

Next to him stood a well-dressed old gentleman also peering at the window. He had a kind and cheerful face.

'Are you searching for a job, sir?' Nicholas asked.

'Me? No,' said the cheerful man. 'But you are looking for one, perhaps?'

Nicholas admitted that he was. There was something so open and friendly about the older man that Nicholas found him very easy to talk to. His name was Charles Cheeryble. He insisted that Nicholas should come with him to his office.

The office was in a quiet square near the Bank of England. On the door of the office was a sign that read: CHEERYBLE BROTHERS.

Nicholas was introduced to Charles's brother, Ned. They were identical in every way, right down to their cheerful, smiling faces.

The twins had come to London years ago.

'At first, we were so poor that we had to go without shoes,' said Charles.

Ned nodded, 'But look at us now!' He and Charles seemed delighted and amazed that they had come so far in the world.

The kind and hard-working Cheeryble Brothers were as different from Ralph Nickleby as anyone could be. They were generous, not mean. They wanted to spend the money they made not on themselves but to do good for others. And, as it happened, they were looking for a new clerk to join the business.

They asked Nicholas to start immediately and offered his family a home. They owned a little cottage on the outskirts of London and said that the Nicklebys (and Smike) were welcome to stay as long as they liked.

Nicholas was happy in his new life. He even met a woman called Madeline Bray, who was a client of the Cheeryble brothers. She was beautiful and kind, and Nicholas grew very fond of her.

A Fright
for Smike

The Cheeryble brothers often
visited the little cottage where
the Nicklebys lived. Every now
and then, their nephew would
visit too. His name was Frank
Cheeryble and like his uncles, he
was generous, open and cheerful.
Frank grew very close to Kate
Nickleby, and she to him.

But while his family had been
living happily on the outskirts of

London, Ralph Nickleby had been plotting. He wanted revenge.

One evening, the Nicklebys and Smike were at home with Frank Cheeryble. The sky had grown dark and the moon sat snugly between the cotton-like clouds. Frank was preparing to leave when suddenly there came a loud knocking at the door.

Nicholas did not even have time to stand before three men stormed in.

He recognised two of them: his uncle Ralph and Mr Squeers.

The third, however, was a short man with a sharp nose. He looked undeniably cruel, but not like anyone Nicholas knew.

'What are you doing here?' said Nicholas.

'I am giving a son back to his father,' said Ralph, looking at Smike.

'This gentleman here is Mr Snawley,' said Mr Squeers. 'He is Smike's father.'

Nicholas remembered the
two miserable boys setting off to
Dotheboys Hall. The man with the
sharp nose must be their father …
Could he be Smike's too?

As if to prove it, the man made straight for Smike and grabbed him by the arm.

'Got him! Oh, I've got him! My own flesh and blood!' cried Mr Snawley.

Nicholas's mind whirled in confusion. 'It can't be true,' he cried.

'We have letters and documents to prove it,' said Ralph.

Mr Snawley let go of Smike and he limped across to his friend.

'I – I don't want to go, Nicholas. P-p-please.'

'I want my son,' said Mr Snawley.

'Your son,' replied Nicholas, 'can choose for himself. He has chosen to stay here with us, and he shall.'

Ralph, Mr Squeers and Mr Snawley glared at Nicholas, who stood there with clenched fists.

Eventually, the three men turned to leave, but not before giving a final threat.

'Watch your back, Smike,' Ralph

said. 'I'll get you sooner or later.'

Nicholas soon realised that Ralph's plan to take Smike was only in order to get revenge on *him*.

Smike had never been strong. Years of neglect and bad treatment had seen to that. Now, with the shock of seeing Squeers again, Smike fell ill.

Nicholas decided to take him to Devonshire, where he and Kate had grown up. He hoped that the peace and quiet of the countryside might help Smike's recovery.

By the time Nicholas and Smike reached Devon, autumn had fallen. The trees were rich with golden leaves, yet the meadows were still as lush and green as Nicholas remembered them being.

Smike enjoyed his time in the countryside, but it was not having the effect they had hoped for – Spike was not getting better. Like the autumn leaves, he was slowly fading away. Soon, he no longer had the strength to walk or even rise from his bed. Yet still he was happy, to be with Nicholas.

The two friends spent endless hours talking, laughing and telling each other stories. Nicholas stayed by Smike's side until the end.

After Smike's death, Nicholas returned to London. A lot had happened while he had been away.

Mr Squeers and Mr Snawley had been arrested for forging the letters that tried to prove Mr Snawley was Smike's father.

After they heard of Mr Squeers's arrest, all the miserable boys at Dotheboys Hall rejoiced – they were free!

First, they forced Mrs Squeers to drink some of the horrible treacle mixture that she fed to them every morning. Then they ran away from that long, drab-looking house on the Yorkshire moors and never looked back.

Newman Noggs had been busy too. He had discovered the truth about Smike's father. He wasn't Mr Snawley, of course. Smike's real father was, in fact, Ralph Nickleby!

Many years ago, Ralph Nickleby had been married. He had married a woman who was set to inherit a fortune from her family – he had hoped to become a rich man, possibly even richer than he was now. But it did not take his new wife long to discover exactly what sort of man Ralph was. He was cruel and greedy, and she could not stand him.

She ran away, even though she was expecting a baby.

The baby was born, but not wanted. Young Smike reminded his mother too much of her horrid husband, and so, he was sent off to Dotheboys Hall.

Ralph Nickleby never knew he was a father. He certainly had no idea that he was the father of poor Smike. When Newman Noggs told him, Ralph felt – probably for the first time in his life – ashamed.

All Ralph's plans had failed: his money-lending business was falling apart, and his plot to gain revenge against his nephew had gone horribly wrong. Not even his precious piles of money could comfort him now.

Ralph Nickleby was in despair.

He went back to his great house in Golden Square. He locked and bolted the doors. He closed the curtains. He climbed the stairs to the top of the house, opened the attic door and locked himself inside. And there, in his dusty attic, surrounded by old furniture and piles of paperwork, he withered away, like a rotting apple.

Fortunately, there is some good that comes from this tragic tale.

The Nicklebys were together once more, living amidst the rolling greens and seaside towns of their beloved Devon.

While Nicholas had been away, Frank Cheeryble had proposed to Kate and the pair were now happily married. Nicholas also found love in the form of Madeline Bray, the kind and beautiful woman he met when working as a clerk for the Cheeryble brothers.

Over the years, more changes came. Nicholas was made business partner in the Cheerybles' company, which was now named: Cheeryble and Nickleby. Kate and Frank, and Nicholas and Madeline had children of their own, and Newman Noggs became like a grandfather to them all.

But, even as time moved on and his family grew and changed, Nicholas still took the time to gaze at the merry meadows outside his window and remember his best friend, Smike.

Charles Dickens

Charles Dickens was born in Portsmouth in 1812. Like many of the characters he wrote about, his family were poor and his childhood was difficult. As an adult, he became known around the world for his books. He is remembered as one of the most important writers of his time.

Ludovic Salle

Born in France, Ludovic graduated from design school and studied visual communication. And now he is free to use a variety of styles, from cartoons to realistic drawings. Ludovic, who likes to think outside of his stereotypes and enjoy adventure, likes to show off his creativity by jumping into new projects such as illustrations, comics, children's books, and exhibitions without hesitation.

NICHOLAS NICKLEBY

초판 1쇄 발행 2023년 6월 27일

글 찰스 디킨스 | 그림 루도빅 살레

ISBN 979-11-6581-436-6 (74840)
ISBN 979-11-6581-418-2 (세트)

발행처 주식회사 스푼북 | 발행인 박상희 | 총괄 김남원
편집 김선영·박선정·김선혜·권새미 | 디자인 조혜진·김광휘 | 마케팅 손준연·이성호·구혜지
출판신고 2016년 11월 15일 제2017-000267호
주소 (03993) 서울시 마포구 월드컵북로 6길 88-7 ky21빌딩 2층
전화 02-6357-0050(편집) 02-6357-0051(마케팅)
팩스 02-6357-0052 | 전자우편 book@spoonbook.co.kr

제품명 Nicholas Nickleby
제조자명 주식회사 스푼북 | **제조국명** 대한민국 | **전화번호** 02-6357-0050
주소 (03993) 서울시 마포구 월드컵북로6길 88-7 ky21빌딩 2층
제조년월 2023년 6월 27일 | **사용연령** 8세 이상
※ KC마크는 이 제품이 공통안전기준에 적합하였음을 의미합니다.

⚠ 주 의

아이들이 모서리에 다치지
않게 주의하세요.